*To the Young family, especially the young Youngs:*
*Becca, Lottie and Martha. Also to Fred and Leo – R.A*

MRS PIG'S NIGHT OUT
by Ros Asquith and Selina Young
British Library Cataloguing in Publication Data.
A catalogue record of this book is available from
the British Library

ISBN 0 340 81707 0 (HB)
ISBN 0 340 81708 9 (PB)

Text copyright © Ros Asquith 2003
Illustrations copyright © Selina Young 2003

The right of Ros Asquith to be identified as
the author of this Work and of Selina Young
to be identified as the illustrator of this Work
has been asserted by them in accordance with
the Copyright, Designs and Patents Act 1988.

First edition published 2003
10 9 8 7 6 5 4 3 2 1

Published by Hodder Children's Books,
a division of Hodder Headline Limited,
338 Euston Road, London NW1 3BH

Printed in Hong Kong

# Mrs Pig's Night Out

Written by Ros Asquith

Illustrated by Selina Young

Hodder
Children's
Books

A division of Hodder Headline Limited

Mrs Pig was going out.

"When will you be back, Mum?" said Big Piggy.
"When you're fast asleep," said Mrs Pig.

"When will you be back, Mum?" said Middle Piggy.
"When you're fast asleep," sighed Mrs Pig.

"When will you be back, Mum?" said Little Piggy.
"When you're fast asleep," groaned Mrs Pig.

# "Oh Mum, don't go out,"

said Little Piggy, Middle Piggy and Big Piggy, all together.

"Goodness me," groaned Mrs Pig. "Daddy will look after you. It's not as though I'm leaving you with a strange pig sitter. Whatever are you complaining about?"

Mrs Pig unwound Little Piggy from her dress, disentangled Middle Piggy from her hat, told Big Piggy that he was old enough to know better and stomped off downstairs.

"Goodness me! Anyone would think I was leaving them with the big bad wolf!" she said to Mr Pig. "Now, you will be sure to get them into bed nice and early, won't you?"

"Of course," said Mr Pig. "You go off and enjoy yourself."

And off went Mrs Pig, without a backward glance.
Actually, she did have a backward glance and she saw
Big Piggy, Middle Piggy and Little Piggy waving at the
upstairs window, with tears streaming down their snouts.

"Dear, oh dear," thought Mrs Pig.

The minute Mrs Pig had disappeared from sight,
the three little pigs ran downstairs.

"Let's have a pillow fight, Dad," said Big Piggy.

"Oh, all right," sighed Mr Pig. "But just one short one.
Then it's bedtime."

They had five quite long pillow fights.

"Bedtime," said Mr Pig.

"But it's Pig Parade on TV," said Big Piggy. "Mum always lets me watch it."

"Oh, all right," said Mr Pig. "Then it's bedtime."

"And I've got to do my tables. Listen to me doing my five times tables," said Middle Piggy.

"Just once," said Mr Pig. "Then it's bedtime."

"Let me do just one drawing," said Little Piggy.

"Just one," said Mr Pig.

# "Then it's bedtime."

And Mr Pig sat down in his favourite armchair and went to sleep.

Big Piggy watched Pig Parade, Dr Pig and Pig-in-a-Poke. Middle Piggy watched too, which was better than saying her five times tables to a sleeping pig. Little Piggy drew eighteen pictures of space rockets and five giant squid.

All three little pigs did portraits of Mr Pig snoring.

"Dad, wake up," said Little Piggy. "We've done your portraits."
"Whatever is the time?" said Mr Pig. "Definitely bedtime!
Quick!"

"Just one more pillow fight,"

said Big Piggy, Middle Piggy and
Little Piggy all together.
"Oh, all right," sighed Mr Pig.
"But just one short one...

...then bedtime!"

They had one rather long pillow fight.
Then they heard Mrs Pig's shoes crunching up
the gravel path.

"Quick, quick, quick!" shouted Mr Pig.

"But we haven't cleaned our teeth," squealed the three little pigs.

"Never mind!
BEDTIME!"

And the three little pigs scampered up the stairs and
dived under the covers – just as Mrs Pig came in.

Mrs Pig looked around. She saw lots of feathers. She saw a large pile of drawings, including some interesting ones of Mr Pig, apparently asleep. She noticed that the TV was on the Piglet channel, which Mr Pig never watched.

She went upstairs and peered round the piglets' door. She went to kiss them and noticed that Little Piggy was not tucked in. As she tucked him in, she also noticed that he had all his clothes on...
So did Middle Piggy... So did Big Piggy...

Mrs Pig went downstairs.

"Did you have a nice evening?" asked Mr Pig, a little nervously.
"Lovely, thank you," said Mrs Pig. "And, isn't it wonderful, the children are all fast asleep and none of their clothes are lying on the floor. You have done well!"

"Oh, it was nothing," blushed Mr Pig.